8-3-01

Beady Bear

BEADY BEAR

STORY AND PICTURES BY DON FREEMAN

PUFFIN BOOKS

For

Marjorie Rankin

of the Children's Room

of the Santa Barbara Public Library

PUFFIN BOOKS

A Division of Penguin Books USA Inc.
375 Hudson Street, New York, New York 10014
Penguin Books Ltd, 27 Wrights Lane, London W8 5TZ England
Penguin Books Australia Ltd, Ringwood, Victoria, Australia
Penguin Books Canada Ltd, 10 Alcorn Avenue, Toronto, Ontario, Canada M4V 3B2
Penguin Books (N.Z.) Ltd, 182-190 Wairau Road, Auckland 10, New Zealand

Penguin Books Ltd, Registered Offices: Harmondsworth, Middlesex, England

First published by The Viking Press 1954
Viking Seafarer Edition published 1971
Reprinted 1974
Published in Picture Puffins 1977

19   20

Copyright Don Freeman, 1954
All rights reserved

Library of Congress Cataloging in Publication Data
Freeman, Don.   Beady Bear.
Summary: A toy bear goes off to a cave to live as a real bear should,
only to find he needs something more to be truly happy.
[1. Toys—Fiction] I. Title.
[PZ8.9.F85Be6]   [E]   76-50658
ISBN 0-14-050197-5

Manufactured in the U.S.A.

Set in Lydian

Beady was a fuzzy toy bear who belonged to a boy named Thayer.

Hide-and-seek was their favorite fun.

From time to time Beady would suddenly stop and topple over—
kerplop! He'd come unwound!

Then Thayer would always go find him and take his key and gently wind him.

8

Once Beady was all wound up, he wanted to keep on playing.

And yet when Thayer went to bed Beady knew he ought to, too.

One winter's day Thayer went away. Just when he'd be back he didn't say.

Being all alone for the first time, Beady amused himself by looking at a book.

"Why hasn't anybody told me this before?" said Beady
sadly to himself.

"I wonder if there could be a cave for me away up in those hill

Taking a long look through Thayer's shiny telescope he searched
the side of the hill until — he spied

a cave!

So he left a note.

Up the hill he climbed and climbed.

At last!

He could hardly believe his beady eyes — it was just his size!

"A perfect place for a brave bear like me!" sighed Beady.

"And yet it's awfully dark and stilly here inside! And a wee bit chilly, really!"

That night Beady couldn't sleep a wink. "It's because of these sharp stones, I think.

"There's something I need in here to make me truly happy.
I wonder what it could be?"

"Oh, I know!" and up he got and out he trotted down the snowy hillside to his house far below.

And what should he bring back but his very own little pillow!

"This is more like it!" said Beady as he bedded down for the rest of the night.

"But there still seems to be something missing!"

So down the hill he trotted again

and brought back—of all things—a flashlight. But as soon as he settled down he knew

there was something more a bear needed to be truly happy.
"What good is a light without something to read?" said Beady.

The evening papers, indeed!

Now what more could a bear ask for?

Well, after reading all the papers, Beady began to worry and wonder. "Maybe it's some toys I need..."

At this very moment he heard a loud noise outside.
"It's a bear!" said Beady.

"I must be brave! This is probably his cave!"

The noise grew louder and louder as Beady moved along, ever
so slowly and shakily. Suddenly he came to a stop —

and over he toppled — kerplop! "Who's there?" cried Beady, upside down.

"It's me, Thayer! I'm looking for my bear!"

But from inside the cave now came not a sound — Beady was
much too embarrassed, lying there on the ground!

"Well, hello, Beady boy! I thought I'd find you in this place.
That's why I brought along your key, just in case!

"For goodness' sakes, Beady, don't you know you need a key?

"And me?"

"Yes, but if I need you, who do you need?"

"I need Beady!"

So down the hill to home they went, paw in hand and hand in paw,

and when Beady went to bed that night, he was the truly
happiest bear you ever saw.